In which we read about Rabbit

One warm spring morning, Rabbit knew that it was going to be one of his busy days.

"It is just the day for doing things," he said, scratching his whiskers. He decided he would walk across the Forest to visit his great friend, Pooh Bear.

Just as he said that, though, a voice called out:

"Is anyone at home?"

Winnie-the-Pooh and Friends
Rabbit

EGMONT
We bring stories to life

This edition published in Great Britain in 2013
by Dean, an imprint of Egmont UK Limited
The Yellow Building, 1 Nicholas Road, London W11 4AN
2013 Disney Enterprises, Inc
Based on the Winnie-the-Pooh works by A. A. Milne and E. H. Shepard
Illustrations by Andrew Grey
Text by Emily Stead

ISBN 978 0 6035 6877 0
55634/1
Printed in Italy

Meet Rabbit

If Rabbit were to introduce himself, he would say he was a

 Very Important Animal

who is happiest when he's organizing something.

He likes **busy days** much better than ones where you **do nothing**. And with so many friends-and-relations to look after, Rabbit's days are very busy indeed!

In this book, you can meet Rabbit and his relatives and listen to a story all about what happens to Rabbit on one of his busy days.

Rabbit
decided
he was
far too busy
for visitors
and called back,

"Nobody is
at home."

"But, isn't that you,
Rabbit?" called the
voice again.

Rabbit thought to himself, then replied that Rabbit
had gone to visit his friend, Pooh.

"But this is Pooh!" said the voice,
sounding very surprised.

So Rabbit invited him in for some tea.

Rabbit got out the plates and mugs and offered Pooh some honey or condensed milk to have with his bread.

Pooh, who was careful to visit his friends around **eleven o'clock,** was very pleased to be offered a little something.

Before long, Pooh had eaten everything in the dishes, and said to Rabbit in a rather **sticky** voice that he must be going.

Pooh pushed his nose and paws through the hole that was Rabbit's front door, but his tummy wouldn't follow.

"Oh, bother!" sniffed Pooh. "I'm stuck."

So Rabbit went out of his back door, and walked round to see Pooh. Rabbit tut-tutted at the Silly Old Bear.

"Give me your paw, Pooh," he said.

Rabbit **pulled** and **pulled** and **pulled**, but Pooh was too tightly stuck. A tear rolled down Pooh's cheek.

"I shall go and fetch Christopher Robin," said Rabbit, and trotted off hurriedly.

Before long, Rabbit returned with Christopher Robin.
"There's only one thing to be done," said Christopher
Robin, solemnly. "We shall have to wait for you to get thin
again, so we can pull you out."

Poor old
Pooh!

He would
have to stay
in the hole
without any
food for a
whole week!

So each day for a week, Christopher Robin came to read stories at the **North end** of Pooh, while Rabbit kept busy in his house at the **South end** of Pooh.

At first, Rabbit was rather annoyed that he couldn't use his front door. But when he discovered how useful Pooh's back legs were for drying his washing, he soon cheered up!

At the end of the week, Christopher Robin told
hold of Pooh's front paws, and Rabbit and all his friends-
and-relations lined up behind.

They all pulled together, and then suddenly
out came Pooh, with a

"Pop!"

Pooh waved
goodbye to his friends
and walked home
through the forest,
humming a little
hum to himself.

Rabbit turned to
Christopher Robin
and said: "You and I have Brain,
Others just have fluff."

Christopher Robin smiled.
"Silly old Bear!"
he said, looking after Pooh.

The next morning, it was Rabbit who was visiting Pooh. He hurried through the Hundred Acre Wood, feeling more important with each step, until soon he came to Pooh's house.

Rabbit knocked at the door loudly.

"Hallo, Pooh," said Rabbit.

"Hallo, Rabbit," said Pooh. Then, "Was it fourteen or fifteen? Bother!"

"Was what?" said Rabbit.

"My pots of honey," sighed Pooh. "I was counting."

"Let's call it sixteen," said Rabbit, kindly.

"Now I came here to ask if you have you seen Small anywhere about?"

Pooh thought to himself, then thought some more, then said: "Who is Small?"

"He's one of my friends-and-relations," said Rabbit carelessly.

This made Pooh even more muddled as to whether he had seen Small round and about, as Rabbit had so many friends-and-relations.

"Well no one has seen Small for a long time," said Rabbit. "So I promised Christopher Robin that I would organize a search."

And that's just what Rabbit did. Before long, he had gathered together as many of his friends-and-relations as he could find.

Hedgehogs, squirrels, mice and smaller rabbits all wanted to help look for Small.

Rabbit lined them up and said importantly: "Small is Lost. We must begin the Search at once."

Rabbit then asked Christopher Robin to explain to

all the animals where and when it was exactly that Small had gone missing.

"Small was taking some exercise, walking around a gorse-bush, when he didn't come back again."

"Ha!" said Rabbit. "Did he say 'goodbye' before he went?"

"I don't think so," said Christopher Robin.

"Lost!" said Rabbit.

A little later, Pooh left his house to join the Search for Small. Not remembering that Small was a Very Small Beetle, Pooh decided to first look for Piglet, who would tell him what Small looked like.

Then Pooh would know whether he ought to be looking for Small

high up

in an oak-tree,

or down low

in a buttercup.

Pooh found Piglet in a funny place indeed and quite by accident – in the bottom of a pit for **Heffalumps!** There they stayed worrying about whether a Heffalump might appear until Christopher Robin came to help them out again.

Then suddenly, Piglet spotted Small, climbing
up Pooh's back. "You have found Small!" squeaked Piglet.

"I thought I had," said Pooh.

"We must tell Rabbit!" said Piglet, rather excitedly,
and ran off to find him straight away.

Two days later, Rabbit was taking one of his brisk walks in the Forest, when he happened to bump into Eeyore.

"Hello, Eeyore," he said. "What are you doing?"

"I'm looking for Small," said Eeyore, in his usual gloomy way.

"Didn't I tell you?" said Rabbit. "Small was found two days ago, by Pooh!"

Now on days when Rabbit wasn't quite so busy and when he didn't have things to organize, he liked to join his friends in a game of Poohsticks.

Rabbit was always the one who said "Go!" and then everyone would drop their sticks in the river and run to the other side of the bridge to see whose stick would come out first.

One sunny day, four friends were playing the game.

"Can you see your stick, Piglet?" cried Roo, who was very excited. "Can you see yours, Pooh? I can't see mine!"

"They always take longer than you think," said Rabbit, wisely.

"I can see a sort of greyish one," said Pooh. "Look, Rabbit, here it comes!"

Then out floated Eeyore from under the bridge, with his legs in the air.

"It's Eeyore!" cried everybody.

"We didn't know you were playing!" called Roo, to Eeyore in the river.

"Wrong," Eeyore replied. "I'm waiting for someone to help me out of the river."

"But Eeyore, how will we do that?" wondered Winnie-the-Pooh.

"He's going **round** and **round!**" smiled Roo.

"I didn't want to go swimming today," sighed Eeyore.

Rabbit scratched his whiskers and and tried to think of a plan.

But it was
Pooh who had
an idea, though
he wasn't sure
whether it was
a very good one.

"If we threw
a big stone
into the river, then it would make waves and wash
Eeyore to the side" said the Bear of Little Brain.

"That's a very good idea," said Rabbit, and Pooh
cheered up.

So Pooh went to look for the biggest stone he
could find.

When Rabbit had inspected it, Pooh held the stone
between his paws and carried it to the bridge.

"Now when I say so, Pooh will drop his stone,"
said Rabbit.

"Thank you, Rabbit," said Pooh.

"Stand back, Piglet," said Rabbit, taking charge.

"Give Pooh some more room.

Ready . . .

Now!"

Pooh dropped his stone into the river below.
There was a **splash!** Then Eeyore disappeared . . .

Rabbit, Pooh, Piglet and Roo looked on from the bridge. They began to worry, then suddenly, something big and grey appeared, and there he was . . .

"Poor Eeyore, you are all wet!" said Piglet.

"Why were you in the river?" asked Rabbit, drying Eeyore with Piglet's handkerchief. "Did you fall in?"

"No," said Eeyore. "I was BOUNCED."

Then from behind the hedge, out came Tigger.

"Hello, everybody!" he smiled.

"Now," said Rabbit, in a very important voice. "What just happened?"

"Just when?" said Tigger.

"When you **bounced** me into the river," said Eeyore.

"It wasn't a bounce, it was a cough," said Tigger, sounding cross.

"It was a **bounce**," said Eeyore.

Eeyore was grumbling that bouncing was very different from coughing and he really would know the difference, when Christopher Robin came out of the Forest, feeling happy and careless.

Rabbit held up his paw. "Hush!" he said. "What does Christopher Robin think?"

Christopher Robin was not quite sure so he decided they should play another game of Poohsticks.

So that's what they did. And Eeyore, who had never played before, won more times than anyone else.
Then later on, Kanga took Roo home to bed, and Tigger and Eeyore followed. And Rabbit, who didn't much like playing Poohsticks when he wasn't winning, decided to go home too.

But Christopher Robin, Pooh and Piglet stayed behind for just one more game . . .

Facts about Rabbit

Rabbit lives to the north of the Hundred Acre Wood, and just south of the sandy pit where Roo plays.

Rabbit is clever and, like Owl, has Brain. Pooh, Piglet and the Others just have fluff.

He likes busy days where he organizes things or writes notices signed Rabbit.

☕ *Rabbit has the most friends-and-relations in the Hundred Acre Wood,* made up of other rabbits, hedgehogs and beetles.

☕ *If Rabbit had a pocket* to carry each member of his family, he would need seventeen pockets!

☕ *Christopher Robin is fond of Pooh* and Piglet and Eeyore, but it is Rabbit on whom he depends (or so Rabbit thinks).

☕ *Rabbit always keeps some condensed milk*, honey and bread in his larder for when Pooh visits.

☕ *When Pooh Bear got stuck in Rabbit's front door,* Rabbit used Pooh's back legs to dry his towels on!

☕ *Unlike Pooh, Rabbit never lets things come to him* – he goes and fetches them.

A Poem about Rabbit
(by Pooh Bear)

I often make a habit,
Of calling to see Rabbit,
When my tummy says it's time
To stop for tea.

There's always bread and honey,
All sticky, sweet and runny,
Rabbit keeps some in his larder
Just for me.

And when there is no more,
I shake Rabbit by the paw,
And think how dear a friend
he is to me.

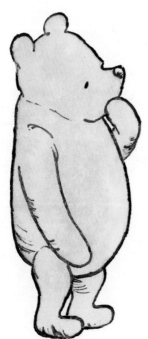